Hired For
Their Pleasure
A Late Bloomer's 1st time

I0547813

JACK RYDER

WARNING

This book contains sexually explicit scenes and adult language. It may be considered offensive to some readers. This book is for sale to adults ONLY.

* * * * * * * * * * * * * * * * * * *

Please store your files wisely where they cannot be accessed by underage readers.

Please feel free to send me an email. Just know that these emails are filtered by my publisher. Good news is always welcome.

Jack Ryder - **jack_ryder@awesomeauthors.org**

You might also want to check my blog for Updates and interesting info.
jack-ryder.awesomeauthors.org

About the Publisher
4Fun Publishing, a member of **BLVNP Incorporated**, 340 S. Lemon #6200, Walnut CA 91789, info@blvnp.com / legal@blvnp.com
NOTE: Due to the highly emotional reaction of some people to works of erotic fiction, any email sent to the above address that contains foul language or religious references is automatically deleted by our anti-spam software and will not be seen. All other communications are welcome.

DISCLAIMER
Please don't be stupid and kill yourself. This book is a work of FICTION. Do not try any new sexual practice that you find in this book. It is fiction and not to be confused with reality. Neither the author nor the publisher or its associates assume any responsibility for any loss, injury, death or legal consequences resulting from acting on the contents in this book. Every character in this book is over 18 years of age. The author's opinions are not to be construed as the opinions of the publisher. The material in this book is for entertainment purposes ONLY. Enjoy.

Hired For Their Pleasure

A Late Bloomer's First Time

Hot Erotica

By: Jack Ryder

© Jack Ryder 2014
ISBN: 978-1-68030-107-6

Chapter 1

The Rhonan's were exactly the sort of family that I grew to despise when I was growing up. Rich, privileged and snooty. The practiced sort of snooty where they could smile in your face and say something that could sound like a compliment while reminding you of your "place." But the sweet sugary words would quickly turn venomous if a young fella like me showed up for a date with their daughter.

Then, the parents would have no problem telling me very plainly that a trailer trash boy like me could never be good enough for their daughter. I would be ushered to the entry gate and told to never darken their doorstep again. In my high school years, I was even roughed up a bit by a couple of overzealous chauffeurs who wanted to be sure that I got the message.

As a quirk of fate, the trailer court that I grew up in was just inside the city boundary where most of the very affluent families lived. As a result, I went to the same schools with the rich kids from elementary school through high school. Needless to say, dating was a miserable experience for me during those years. Even the girls of my same social station would shy away because they had their minds geared to improving their situation. They wanted to escape the trailer trash stigma.

***

It's a bit embarrassing to tell you that I was still a virgin the day I enlisted in the US Army. This 6 foot 4 "Army of One" had never even had a blowjob up to this point in life. Although my grades in school had not been good enough to qualify me for any sort of college scholarship, they were way good enough for Uncle Sam's army. My maintenance aptitude scores were off the charts as were my cognitive skills scores. Something they called lateral thinking.

I spent my first three years in Afghanistan dodging sniper bullets as we tried to clear out the endless system of caves and tunnels where the enemy had dug in. During those years I fought hard, drank hard and played whenever the opportunity presented itself. I finally lost my cherry in a concrete bunker to a cute little PFC named Bernie. Her real name was Bernadette, but she preferred the abbreviated version.

It was my twentieth birthday and Bernie and I got saddled together to hold down the bunker while the rest of our squad pressed forward to pursue a known terrorist leader. We were told to hold the position until more supplies arrived, which were needed to continue further into the mountains. Bernie was a cute little thing. Of course, since I am 6 foot 4, pretty much any girl I know could be classified as a little thing.

Bernie was always friendly towards me. I think that was mainly due to the fact that I was the only one in camp that did not refer to her as "BJ." Except, of course, our commanding officer. Since her last name is Jones, you can see how she got stuck with the unfortunate nickname. But the worst part was that most of the other guys were hoping she would live up to her name. That kept her at odds with them when they tried to schmooze her. Especially, when drinking was involved.

It was a very dark moonless night. It had been a very hot day with the temperature reaching over 124F. It was still near ninety as midnight approached. Both of us had stripped off our vests and long sleeve shirts and were only wearing our sweat soaked desert tan t-shirts. There were several times over the course of the evening that my eyes gazed at her lovely round tits pressed against the moist cotton shirt. I felt a little stirring between my legs and quickly forced myself to occupy my mind with other tasks.

"What was that card that you got from your mother the other day?" She asked me casually while we were having a late snack before turning in for the night. "It was a birthday card," I answered her. "Really?" She exclaimed. "Yes, but my birthday was really today," I informed her. "Really," she asked again. "Yep, I am twenty years old today," I announced.

"Wow, I would never have guessed that I am a year older than you," she gasped. I noticed that she scooted over closer so that she was practically up against me. "We should do something special to celebrate," she whispered. "Hey, it doesn't get any better than this," I joked. "Here I am at the concrete Hilton with the cutest girl in Afghanistan. How could it get any better than that?" I teased.

Bernie turned to face me and slowly pulled her t-shirt off over her head. "Like this, sweetie." My mouth fell open as her tits sprung free. They were a firm round 34B with coral pink areolas. Her nipples looked like hard pencil erasers. "Oooh, Bernie," I gasped softly. "Go ahead, Jake, touch them if you want," she whispered. My hands trembled slightly as I reached forward to fondle her soft round globes.

"Yessss, that feels nice, Jake," she sighed. I was pleased at how her nipples responded so nicely to my twisting them gently. I could feel her trembling as I rolled them back and forth between my fingers. My dick was rigid and pulsating in my fatigue pants within a few short moments. I moved my head forward and took her left nipple in my mouth and swirled my tongue around her areola and then nibble on the nipple gently. "Yesssssss," Bernie moaned softly.

After sucking on both of her nipples for a few moments, Bernie stood up and took my hand. "I want you to fuck me, Jake," she told me softly. She led me over to the cot in the corner and pushed me back till I was seated in the middle of the small bed. He breasts looked beautiful as she bent down to remove my combat boots and socks. "Now, it's your turn," she told me as she sat down next to me.

I crawled off the bed and quickly untied her boots and pulled them off. As I was pulling off her socks, Bernie removed her belt and unbuttoned her fatigue pants. "May as well take these off too," she giggled playfully. She lifted her ass so I could pull her pants down and I slowly peeled them down to her knees. She was wearing a pair a soft pink boy shorts panties underneath.

"Oh Bernie, look at you," I groaned softly. The crotch of her panties were wedged slightly into her pussy lips allowing me to see the contour of her labia.

"Okay, YOUR turn," she laughed as she stood up off the bed. Bernie slowly removed my belt and then started to unbutton my fatigue pants. "I never imagined you were so sexy under all that uniform," I whispered as I glanced up and down her sexy milky white body. She is a true redhead with the creamy white skin and smattering of freckles all over. "Damn, you are pretty," I gasped.

Bernie pushed me back till I was again seated on the army cot. She very slowly pulled my pants down to my ankles and yanked them off over my feet. "What have we here?" she chuckled as she pulled the waist of my undershorts down to expose my throbbing prick. "Ooooh, Jake, that's huge," she gasped as she wrapped her hand around my 9 inch dick. Her hand could barely fit all the way around the girth.

Bernie pulled my underwear off then pushed my knees apart so she could crawl up between my legs. "Ooooh Bernie, Oh My god, Yesss," I groaned as she swirled her tongue around the head of my dick. I was amazed at how she nibbled and sucked on my engorged mushroom and used her tongue to lick every drop of precum that was oozing out.

"Would you like to fuck me for your birthday present," she whispered. "Oh Yes Bernie, Oh Yes," I groaned hoarsely. Without hesitation, Bernie straddled my lap and slowly lowered herself till my dick was pressed against her drenched slit. "Happy birthday, Jake," she whispered. "Oooh, Fuck Yes," I groaned as she thrust straight down till she was impaled on my prick.

"Ooooh, fuck you're huge," Bernie gasped as her body quivered on top of mine. Her pussy was clenched around my cock so tightly that I could feel every molecule of her slick cunt squeezing on my dick. I could feel the pulsations of her heart pressing on me. "Oooh, Fuck Bernie, Fuuck," I groaned. She bent forward and gently kissed my lips as she began to hump back and forth.

"Yessss, Jake, Yes," she purred when I bent forward to suck on one tit and then the other. The sensation of her tight sex hole grinding back and forth on my rigidness was more spectacular than anything I had ever experienced. Bernie was my very first. "It feels so good, Bernie, it feels so fucking good," I moaned between her lovely round breasts.

Because this was my very first time with a woman, I did not last very long at all. It was only a couple of minutes till I felt the stinging in my nutsack that precedes ejaculation. "Oh Bernie, I'm gunna...gunna...OH MY GOD YES...OH FUCK YES," I yelled as my dick exploded into her pussy over and over. "Oooooh, Jaaaaaaaake," she moaned throatily as her body quivered into climax too.

I was amazed at the amount of semen that drooled out of her gash when she rolled off of me to squeeze her body next to mine on the small army cot. "I'm sorry I didn't last longer," I told her as she draped her left leg over mine and laid her head on my chest. "Don't be silly. We both needed a good frantic hump," she chuckled her reply. "We can do the long passionate thing after we rest awhile," she added as she gently kissed the side of my neck.

We both fell asleep within a few minutes all cuddle together with her head on my chest and leg draped over the top of mine. It was the twilight just before dawn that I awoke and felt her hand gently fondling my manhood. "That was incredible last night. It was my first," I whispered to her.

"Yeah, you're the first one I had since I deployed over here too," she answered. "You are the only one that has treated me with respect and didn't try to get in my pants," she added as she craned her head up to kiss my cheek.

"No, you were my very first." I could feel the blood of embarrassment rushing into my cheeks.

"Jaaaaaake, that is...so precious!" she squealed. Before I could say another word, she scooted on top of me and had her tongue halfway down my throat. "I will never forget this, Jake," she gasped when she finally let us take a breath. Her pussy was dripping as she ground herself against my swelling dick.

"I think it's time we had round two," she whispered in my ear when she felt my dick throbbing against her drenched sex. "Yes, I think we should," I laughed as I rolled her on her back so I could be on top this time. "Ooooooh, Fuck yes," she moaned as I slowly shoved my dick into her hot wet hole till I was buried to the root.

I raised up with my arms so I could see every inch of her sexy milky white body as I seesawed my dick in and out of her. It fascinated me to see her pussy lips stretch outward each time my cock pulled out and then pressed back in as I thrust forward. "Fuck me, Jake, Fuck me," she moaned in a deep husky voice.

Smack, Smack, Smack, Smack...the sound of my belly slapping down against Bernie's echoed off the concrete bunker walls. Ugh, Ugh, Ugh...her soft grunts as I pounded into her thrilled me even more. All these sounds and new sensations filled me with a giddiness and arousal that was beyond anything I could ever remember. "Fill me with your cum, Jake...fill my pussy with cum," she groaned.

The musky scent of her sex added to the nastiness of her words made me intoxicated with arousal. I pounded into Bernie harder and faster as I felt her body beginning to vibrate beneath me. As I felt the load building up in my balls, I shoved harder and harder to get my dick as far inside of her as I could. "HERE IT IS, HERE IT IS, BABY," I screamed as I sprayed my semen deep into her womb. Bernie wrapped her legs around my waist and kept me buried inside till my dick finally went soft and fell out of her cum filled gash.

***

Bernie and I secretly fucked each other about a dozen times or so over that final year that we were in Afghanistan together. I never saw her again after she rotated home to the US and I was reassigned to a unit in Germany. There is no way that I will ever forget her, our very special first night together or the wonderful closeness we shared in that hellhole.

Chapter 2

I saw the advertisement on one of those online job search sites that the workforce officials make you use while you are on unemployment. I wasn't really in too much of a hurry to find a job since I had only been back in the US for less than a month. Six years in the US Army had kept me very busy and I was looking forward to relaxing for a bit before joining the workforce.

The advertisement stated that a very affluent family was looking for a maintenance provider that could take care of all household maintenance concerns as well as grounds keeping. Although the name of the family was not revealed, I recognized the address as one of the mansions up on Knob Hill where the ultra-wealthy folks live.

Because I had to submit at least three work requests each week to show I was actively seeking employment, I decided to answer the ad. I was certain that these rich snobs would never hire a trailer trash guy like me. I sent off a quick bio that outlined my combat experience and the three years of training in Europe as a civil engineer. I also included a photo that was taken by Bernie. It was taken in the little hut where she and I met for sex. I was wearing my fatigue pants and one of those muscle shirt tank tops. I forgot that in the background of that shot you could see Bernie in the mirror taking the photo. She was naked except for a pair of black nylon transparent panties.

I was amazed when I received an invitation to meet with Mrs. Rhonan for a personal interview. The appointment was for noon the next day which was surprising since it would be a Sunday. She also requested that I bring swimming trunks in case she needed me to help her with a project in the Olympic sized pool. "Don't bother wearing a suit and tie," she added. "Jeans and a tank top will do just fine." I had to read the message three times to believe it was real. I must have checked and rechecked her email address a dozen times to make sure it wasn't a hoax of some sort. But it was indeed the same address that I had sent my job request to.

There was a man in a butler's suit that met me at the gate at ten minutes before noon on that sunny Sunday. "Mrs. Rhonan requested that you join her by the pool," he told me as he let me in. "You can park your vehicle in the garage next to the main house and I will come lead you back onto the grounds," he advised.

I was amazed by the size of the garage. It was easily the size of a huge aircraft hangar. There were seven vehicles parked inside and there could easily be another ten with lots of room to spare. Six of those vehicles were restored vintage muscle cars from the 70's.

"Follow me this way, Mr. Dixx," Charles the butler announced when he emerged from a side door that led into the main mansion. He led me through a hallway that took us through the kitchen where there was a three person staff busy with their daily chores. I thought it was quite normal that he would not lead trailer trash like me through the main house. "She's waiting by the pool," Charles told me softly once we were out in the garden area.

The pool must have been at least a hundred yards out. The garden and lawn that led out to the pool was magnificent. So was the 38 year old blonde sitting out by the pool. My eyes were memorizing every inch of her as I approached. She was wearing a one piece bathing suit that covered less of her than most bikinis.

The top tied around her neck and the three inches of material that came down and covered her nipples was white with a black leopard print design. The material did little else to cover her huge 36D silicone globes that stuck out on both sides. There were silver rings at the bottom of both three inch strips that connected to a three inch black strip of material that ran down her belly to the very tiny triangle wedged between her legs that barely covered her gash.

"You must be Jake," she greeted me as I arrived next to her. I made it a point to keep my eyes riveted to hers as I reached out to take her hand. "It's nice to meet you Mrs. Rhonan," I told her softly. "Please, call me, Marissa," she sat up as she said it. "The Mrs. Rhonan thing makes me feel so old and ugly."

I swear I could see the top inch of her gash as she swung her legs around. Then, I could very clearly see her pussy lips poking around the edge of her tiny triangle bottom. "Oh Marissa, you could never be ugly," I gasped softly as I gazed at her nearly nude body. It took every ounce of self-control to keep my dick from springing to life.

"Follow me, Hun," she said as she stood up. I was amazed that her huge jugs didn't fall out of the pathetic little straps. "I have a favor to ask of you," she said it as she grabbed my hand and pulled me over toward the dressing cabana off from the side of the pool. "I forgot the swimming trunks," I informed her timidly as I figured out why she was taking me there. "That's okay, you can just wear your underwear," she giggled. "I do it all the time," she added with a wink.

As I began to undress in the cabana, I was dreading the fact that I chose a very skimpy black thong this morning. It was also very obvious that Marissa was staring at me the entire time I undressed since there was no door on the cabana and she purposely left the curtain open.

"Look at you, Hun," she giggled in a girly tone as her eyes raked up and down my body. "You look even better in person than in that photo you sent."

I felt practically naked as she led me out to the pool. It was extremely difficult to keep my dick from swelling as I gawked at her silky tan bare ass. The back of her swimsuit was merely a thin string up the crack of her butt. "Oh geezus," I groaned to myself softly as I watched her lovely round ass cheeks jiggle slightly with each step. My dick was fully rigid by the time we reached the pool.

"I'll owe you forever if you can do this for me." She sort of mumbled it. When I glanced up at her face, I saw that she was staring at my cock. My skimpy thong was not enough to keep the head of my nine inch prick from poking up over the waistband. "Oh My," she gasped softly when she looked back up into my eyes.

After she stared at my dick for several more moments, she informed me that her huge diamond wedding ring had come off and slid down to the bottom of the pool. She told me that none of the servants had been able to hold their breath long enough to pull the drain screen out and bring it up with the ring. "So, I guess this is an audition of sorts," I chuckled. "If you can get my ring, you will have the sweetest job of all time," she whispered.

"Be right back," I told her as I walked to the deep end of the pool where the drain would be the closest. I dove straight down and was at the drain within seconds. It took me several moments to figure out that you had to twist the drain counter clockwise in order to remove it. I was back at the surface with the drain screen in hand in less than thirty seconds.

Marissa had climbed into the shallow end of the pool while I was under water. As I a swam towards her with the filter trap in my hand, I saw her pull her top straps apart so her huge round tits were now fully exposed to me. "I was right about you, Jake...you're a keeper," she chuckled as I handed her the trap with her diamond ring cradled inside. I did not try to hide that I was staring at her gorgeous tits.

Almost half of my 9 inch dick was poking out the top of my thong as her hand reached down to fondle it. "I think I owe my new employee a proper reward," she whispered as she reached over to place the drain trap on the ledge next to the pool. "Ooooooh, Fuuuuccck," I groaned softly as her hand pushed my thong down to fully expose my rigidness. When I reached down between her legs, I found that she had pulled the crotch of her suit to the side and her pussy was bare and exposed to my intruding fingers.

"Yessss, Jake, Yessssss," she whispered. I felt her body shudder as I drove two fingers up into her gash. "Ooooh Fuck, Marissa...Oh Fuck," I groaned as her hand jerked up and down my prick. I bent my head down and sucked on one tit and then the other as I drilled my fingers in and out of Marissa's cunt. "Is this part of my duties," I whispered as I kissed up to the side of her neck. "No baby, this is a perk," she laughed. "I'm gunna....love...the perks," I panted as my dick ejaculated my load of cum into the cool water of the swimming pool. "Meeeee toooooo," Marissa moaned as I got her off with my fingers.

We sat on the steps under the water for several minutes while I pulled my thong back up and Marissa pulled her swim suit back in place. "You can take a shower in the cabana before you get dressed," Marissa told me as she began to climb out of the pool. "You can just leave your thong on the floor and I'll see to it that it's returned after it is laundered." she added. I could still feel cum drooling into my thong as I made my way out of the pool. "I'll have Charles show you to my private study," she called to me as she walked towards the mansion. Her ass swaying slightly.

This time, Charles led me into the mansion through the huge French double doors from the outside patio. We passed through a huge drawing room of sorts and into the main entry foyer that was an expansive open area with lots of art on the walls and many tables with various art items on display. Then he led me up a huge double spiral staircase and down a very long hallway till we were at the end of the west wing. "Mrs. Rhonan will join you shortly, sir," he told me as he ushered me into the room on the left.

It was a very large library sort of room but with a definite woman's touch. There were lovely white transparent drapes on the windows, a very nice couch along one wall that had a peach and teal colored pattern to it and everything in the room had a peach and light teal color theme. There was a huge teak wood desk near the entry to the outside patio and a matching teak wood roll top desk against the wall where the book shelves were. There was a large screen laptop on the open shelf of the roll top.

"You like my private playroom?" Marissa asked playfully as she entered the room. I heard the door close as I turned to face her. "My God, you're pretty," I whispered as I gawked at her. The simple light tan summer dress she was wearing was elegantly fitted to her body. The top three buttons were left open which displayed a nice amount of her cleavage and just the top of the black frilly bra that was underneath.

She had left the bottom two buttons unfastened as well. This allowed me to see her lovely long sleek legs as she walked towards me. Even with her flat sandals on, Marissa is nearly 6 foot tall which makes her the tallest woman I have ever been with. At 38 years old she stunning and more gorgeous than most of the women I have ever slept with. Her 36-26-36 figure is pleasantly voluptuous and even though her tits are silicone, they are magnificent.

"Come sit with me," she suggested as she sat down on the couch and crossed her legs. "Let's discuss the details of your employment." Her hand was patting the couch next to her as a small gesture that she wanted me next to her. "I won't bite," she giggled. "Unless you like that sort of thing," she added with a wink. I made my way to her and stood directly in front of her and gazed directly down at her luscious tits.

There is something you need to know about me before you decide to hire me. I did not try to hide the fact I was gawking at her tits. "I'm the sort of guy that you would not let your daughter date when I was a teenager," I growled at her. "I was the trailer trash kid that you would have told Charles to usher to the gate because I wasn't good enough for your little princess. I was the kid that limped home with bruised ribs and a broken heart." I reached down and grabbed ahold of her left tit and squeezed it roughly. "Are you sure you want me to darken your doorway as a hired hand?" I groused at her.

"Ooooh Jake, Yessss, I do," she moaned softly. I could feel her trembling as I continued to fondle her tit a little more gently. "Please, sit down so we can talk," she moaned hoarsely. I gently let go of her breast and sat down next to her. "Tell me what your needs are Jake, and I'll tell you mine," she suggested softly. I felt her hand reach over to rest on top of my thigh. I could feel a slight wiggle between my legs as her fingers gently petted the inside of my thigh.

I told Marissa that I needed enough money to support myself and that I wanted to complete my Master's degree in college. I told her that I could be available during the days but that several nights each week I would be attending classes. I confided that I hoped to earn enough to send some money to help my mother. The entire time I was talking, Marissa continued to pet my thigh with her fingers and they had moved up closer and closer to my swelling prick.

"Are you planning to pursue some sort of civil engineering career?" She asked me softly. Her hand was practically in my crotch now. When I told her that my intent was to become a writer, her hand moved over and gently fondled my cock through the fabric of my jeans. "That's so wonderful," she whispered. "You could stay here and write whenever you desire." I felt a small ooze of precum as her thumb gently rubbed back and forth across the head of my dick.

"I have several needs," she whispered it in my ear as she leaned over to nibble on my earlobe. First, she told me that she would want me to oversee any maintenance or grounds keeping concerns for the entire estate. It would be my job to assess what was needed and then hire the proper people to complete the tasks.

Marissa offered a salary of 50K per year plus living quarters with all utilities and expenses paid. She said that I could make use of their medical and dental professionals at the family expense. She also told me that she would personally pay for my college tuition. In return, I would give her a five year commitment of service with the understanding I could stay as long as I wanted after the commitment was fulfilled.

"I also have some personal needs," she whispered in my ear as her fingers deftly unfastened my belt and began to open my jeans. "My husband has a mistress and I'm tired of having to satisfy certain desires all by myself," she confided. "This would not be a job requirement." She nibbled on my ear as her hand slipped into my pants to grasp my boner. "But I'm certain that I could make you very happy if you would occasionally satisfy those needs," she purred.

"Ooooh Marissa, Oh God Yes, Yesssss," I moaned when she bent down to take my dick into her mouth. "It's all settled then," she giggled as she swirled her tongue around the crown of my cock. "Oooooh, God Yesssss," I groaned as she engulfed my dick again. I reached down and started to unbutton her dress as her head bobbed up and down on my cock.

"I want to fuck you Marissa," I growled as I reached into her dress to fondle her lovely silicone tits. "I want to fuck your right here on this couch," I groaned. When she took her mouth off my prick and sat up, I quickly got on my knees between her legs and unbuttoned the rest of her dress. I was delighted to find that she was not wearing any panties. "You wanted this big dick inside of you, huh?" I taunted her as I drug my dick up and down her sloppy wet gash.

"Yes, Jake, Fuck Me...Fuck Me Please," she moaned in a husky tone. "Oooooh, My God Yes," she howled as I drove my 9 inch dick all the way into her slit until I was buried inside. "Is that what you were needing, baby?" I groaned as I held my dick fully engulf in her sex. "Oh Yes Jake, Oh Thank You...Yessss," she moaned. It thrilled me to see my fat dick stretching and pulling her cunt lips out as I slowly pulled my dick back out.

Part of me relished the fact that I was banging a rich man's wife after all those painful and very humiliating childhood years. But part of me was ecstatic that this gorgeous woman was so filled with desire for me. The expression of sheer lust on her face aroused me deeply. Her low husky moans incited me to satisfy her every need. "Fuck me Jake, Oh God Yes, Fuck Me." Her body quivered as I continued to seesaw my dick in and out of her sex hole.

Marissa was so aroused that her pussy was gushing wet as I began to pound my dick into her harder and harder. I reached forward and pulled on the center of her bra until it ripped open to expose her gorgeous jugs. "Damn, you've got great tits," I groaned as I grabbed them with both hands and squeezed them and pinched on her nipples.

"Take me Jake...Taaaaake Me," Marissa moaned as I felt her body starting to convulse on the couch beneath me. I quickly yanked my dick out of her gash and shoved it between her tits just as I began to ejaculate. "Oh Fuck Yes...Oh My God Yes," I screamed as my semen sprayed all over her big round titties. "Oooooh Jaaaaaake," she whispered as she felt the heat of my slick fluid oozing down her breasts.

Chapter 3

It was 9am when I returned to the Rhonan mansion on Monday morning. I used the special coded remote that Marissa had given me to let myself in the front gate. Although I had been told that I could use the parking garage, I pulled around behind it and parked next to the small cottage where I would be living. There was plenty of room between the back of the garage and the small cottage for my large Humvee. It would be easier to unload my belongings this way.

"Mom said you'd be here at nine." The unexpected voice startled me and I dropped my keys in order to not drop my laptop. "SHIT...YOU EVER HEARD OF PRIVACY?" I yelled as I snapped my head to see where the voice came from. "THAT SHIT WOULD HAVE GOT YOU KILLED IN AFGHANISTAN," I added.

There was a very sexy young blonde sitting on the foot of my bed. I would guess that she is about twenty years old. She looks a clone of that Paris Hilton chick. I would guess that she is 5 foot 8 and probably about a 32A-26-32. Like I said, a slender girl. Although her tiny white bikini covered her adequately, it was easy to see that she is a sexy little thing. I also could see that her nipples were hard as marbles.

"Mom said you might be a little crusty...being trailer trash and all," she answered me. "Yeah, and she said you'd be a snotty self-centered bitch," I replied without hesitation. I sat my laptop on the kitchen table and stepped over in front of her. "Now, are you going to speak to me like a human being or are you going to get out of my house?" I folded my arms across my chest and stared straight down at her.

"Geeeez! Settle down. I was just trying to..." Before she could finish, I cut her off. "You were just trying to remind me of my PLACE," I growled at her. "Before you stick that pointy nose too far in the air, you should consider two things," I was still talking very loudly. I could see that she was starting to squirm a bit with me directly in front of her and between her legs.

"First, you need to respect this trailer trash soldier who fought three years of war in Afghanistan while you were jerking off pimple faced boys here in your cozy little world." I could feel the blood of anger racing to my face. "There were trailer trash boys that died over there that were better human beings than you'll ever be!" Now, I was yelling again.

"And the second thing you need to remember is that I work for your mother, NOT YOU," I spit the words at her. "I don't give a shit if you approve of me or not." I told her. "I will be nice to you, but if you are shitty to me, you can expect the same in return." There was a long silence as she just stared up at me speechless. "I don't ever want to hear the words trailer trash come out of your mouth again," I whispered as I stepped back and went back to the kitchen table.

I was surprised that my hands were trembling a bit as I sat down at my kitchen table. And even more surprised that I now had a full chubby pulsating in my jeans. "WOW!" Kathleen gasped. It sounded like she had been holding her breath and now finally let it out. "I'm sorry, Jake. I didn't mean to get off on the wrong foot with you," she said softly. "I just wanted to see what had my Mom so excited about."

Kathleen got of the bed and walked over to the table. I was thankful that the table was blocking her view of the boner in my pants. "You were right," she whispered. "I should remember that you are a man that deserves respect. You are definitely not like any of the boys that I have ever known." My eyes fell to her perky tits for a moment and I felt a drool of precum as I gawked at her hard nipples pressed against the white fabric of her tiny bikini top.

Kathleen was grinning when I glanced back up. "Maybe we can start over, Jake." My dick was now throbbing painfully as she bent forward slightly to bring her face closer to mine. "I think that you are someone that I would really like to be friends with," she whispered. I noticed that she glanced down into my lap as she said it. Her smile had grown considerably when she stood back up. "I promise to be more...human...from now on."

"I think I'd like that," I answered her as she turned and made her way to the door. "Oooh God," I whispered to myself as I watched her young tight little ass swish back and forth as she walked away. Her tiny little bikini bottom as wedged into the crack of her ass and I could see a good amount of her ass cheeks poking out the sides. "I'm sorry I got so angry," I called after her. She turned and looked back at me. Her eyes were focused beneath the table where she could clearly see my boner. "I think we'll be okay," she replied with a playful chuckle.

***

I just finished unloading all my clothes out of my Hummer when I saw Marissa approaching. She was carrying a covered plate and a large air pot type thermos. "I thought you might like some breakfast," she called to me as she drew closer. She was wearing a soft white summer wrap skirt and a bright blue wrap around short sleeved blouse that was tied in a knot beneath her big yummy tits. "That was very thoughtful," I answered her. There was a tremble in my voice.

"I hear you had words," Marissa told me as we entered my kitchen. "Should I take my things and go home?" I asked in jest. "Oh, Hell no," she chuckled. "I think it was good for her to grow up some," she added. She was smiling as she placed the covered plate into my oven and turned the temperature knob to low. "This might have to be brunch," she giggled. "But you can bring a cup of coffee if you like," she said it as she started walking towards the hallway. "I'll be waiting in the bedroom."

About halfway down the hall, her wrap skirt fell off to the floor. Two steps later, the top followed.

Marissa was nude when she made it to my bedroom and turned to wink at me. I decided that the coffee could wait till later too. "Have I mentioned how fucking sexy you are?" I gasped as I entered my room while tearing my clothes off. "You are pretty damn hot, yourself," she told me as I kicked off my undershorts and jumped onto the bed with her. "Bring that big yummy dick over here," she laughed.

"Ooooooh, Yessssss," Marissa purred when I scooted between her legs and shoved my dick into her in one brutal thrust. I slowly pulled out then pressed back into Marissa while I kissed on the side of her neck. "Ooooh Jake, Ooooh Jake," she moaned. I rose up with my arms so I could watch my dick pounding into her as I slammed down onto her over and over. It aroused me to see her big beautiful tits jiggle each time I thrust into her sex.

"Fill me up, Fill my pussy up," she grunted. I lowered myself and sucked on her tits as I humped into her faster and faster. Her big rubbery nipples felt wonderful in my mouth as I sucked on them and swirled my tongue their rigidness. As I felt the load of cum building up, I raised back up so I could watch her face as I began to ejaculate inside of her. "Here it is baby, here it is," I groaned.

When Marissa felt the scalding heat of my cum flooding into her, she began to writhe and jerk and her face twisted into a lustful mask of rapture. "Oh God yes, Yes, Yesssss," she moaned her reply.

Kathleen was lying out by the pool when Marissa and I came out of my cottage. She was looking directly over at us we came out the door. She even lifted her hand and waved over to us. "Is this going to be a problem?" I whispered softly. "Not at all, sweetie...not at all," Marissa told me softly. "Except that...she may come looking for some too." She said it in an amused tone.

"Really?" I gasped. "And how would that go over?" I asked tentatively. Marissa turned and kissed me on the cheek. "That would depend on you," she whispered inches from my ear. "I certainly won't have a problem with it." She patted me on the ass gently. "Keep me happy and do your job and I'll have no problems with your other business." I stood there shocked as she walked away. I glanced over at

Kathleen and she was smiling broadly at me. Then she casually turned over and put her huge sun glasses on.

After I ate the waffles and scrambled eggs that Marissa had brought over for breakfast, I spent the rest of the morning cleaning my little cottage and moving the furniture around to my liking. I made a list of things I was going to need and then took a quick shower. It was lunch time when my cell phone rang. It was Marissa inviting me over to the main house for lunch. I informed her that I was on my way out the door to do some shopping.

"Maybe you should take Katie with you," Marissa suggested. "She could help you with finding the Mall and other shopping areas," she told me. "Oh, she'll know where Wal-Mart and Target is located," I taunted. "Ba-ha-ha-ha....she'll love that," Marissa burst into laughter. "Do you really think this is a good idea?" I asked her softly. "Yes, I do...it will give her a second chance to get to know you," Marissa advised. "And I will have no problem with anything that happens," she added. "Wow!" I muttered to myself as I hung up the phone. I was further amazed when I glanced out the window and saw Kathleen already coming towards the cottage.

"Are you my guide, my chaperone or my best buddy today?" I teased her as she arrived at my Hummer. "Probably a little of all three," she chuckled her reply. "But I'm hoping to be buddies by the time we return." she added. Katie seemed nicely impressed when I held the door open as she climbed up into the Humvee. "Wow, this is cool," she sighed. "I've never been in one of these before," she confided. "I guess I will be a wealth of new experiences for you, huh?" I chuckled. "Oh, I certainly hope so, Jake." She said it in a coy flirty tone.

"Oooh, Fuck me," I whispered to myself as I climbed into the driver's seat. Katie's blue and white print wrap skirt had fallen open over her left thigh and I could see her entire thigh and the fact that she had no panties on. I could clearly see her smooth shaved gash. The white bikini top that she was still wearing did little to hide that her nipples were again hard as little marbles. "Where to?" I croaked out hoarsely as I snapped my head forward and reached down to start the vehicle.

"That depends, smarty pants," she giggled. "Are we going to Wal-Mart or can I show you where to buy some quality stuff?" I glanced over at her and had to laugh when I saw that she had pulled her top open to expose her tits to me. "Keep that up and we'll be looking for a Motel instead," I teased her. "And those are definitely quality goods," I added.

I was pleasantly surprised with how much fun I had shopping with Kathleen that day. She dragged me all over the local mall and talked me into buying stuff I had not even planned looking at. My main interest had been a new coffee machine for the kitchen and a flat screen TV to hang in my living room. I also wanted to find a new bedspread for my large king sized bed since the one on it now is more for a woman's taste.

By the time we finished shopping, I had two new pair of tight fitting jeans, new swim trunks, four new pair of thong underwear several very nice dress shirts. Katie had taken great pleasure in helping me select these items. She giggled when I tried on what she called "fuddy duddy" items and cooed gleefully when I modeled the items that she selected. She pouted in a playful way when I told her that I could not model the thongs for her. "It will give me something to look forward to," she teased me.

Chapter 4

It was almost dinner time when we returned to the Rhonan Mansion. Katie helped me carry in my shopping bags and then craned her neck to kiss me on the cheek. "Thank you for a wonderful afternoon," she told me. "Yes, it was more fun than I would have guessed," I agreed as she stepped back. "I think we are going to be great buddies," I added. Katie had a goofy look on her face as she gazed up at me. "I better...go," she whispered. "I should...get ready for dinner."

After I put my new clothes away, I took a quick shower and then relaxed on my sofa for a few moments while I tried to envision exactly where I would locate my new TV. I was startled when there was a sudden knock on my front door. Without even thinking about it, I answered the door with just the towel wrapped around my waist.

"Mom asked me to invite you over for dinner," the young girl with short coal black hair informed me. "You must be Stephanie?" I asked while I pulled the towel a little tighter around my waist. "Stevie...my friends call me Stevie," she told me very softly. "Mom said to come as you are."

There was a wry grin on her face as she said it. "I'D LOVE to see that," she added.

Stevie is 18 years old and goes out of her way to dress in a Goth sort of style. Her short wispy pixie sort of hair is shiny black with the last three inches frosted blonde. She has a small ring pierced into her left eyebrow, black lipstick and black fingernail polish. Today, she is wearing olive drab fatigue pants that have been cut off to make shorts. She has a white tank top on that does not hide the fact that she is braless. She finished the look with black combat boots and white knee high socks that were rolled down to the top of her boots.

"Did I know you in Afghanistan?" I teased her as I gazed her at attire. That got a soft giggle. "I take it by the way you dress that YOU are the family rebel." I told her with a smile. "Yes, I am the black sheep." she told me with a small grin. "Perhaps I should at least put some pants on," I told her playfully. "I could wear my combat boots if that would make you feel more comfortable."

Stevie let out a belly laugh. "If you could wear just the boots and no pants...THAT would be something worth seeing at the dinner table," she goaded. I was surprised that she waited while I got dressed. And even more when I saw her peeking at me in the mirror in the hallway.

I had a few moments to gawk at her when I came back out since she had her back to me. I marveled at the difference between her and the older sister. Where Kathleen is a sensuously slender woman, Stevie is a little bombshell that sort of reminds you of that Hayden girl that was on the TV show called Heroes. Her perfectly round 34B tits looked delicious pressed against the white tank top.

"I'm surprised that you waited for me," I told her as we walked towards the house. "Mom said not to come back without you," she replied with a sly grin. "Did you find what you were looking for when I was getting dressed?" I teased her. She had that wry smirk on her face as she glanced up at me but I could see a slight flush in her cheeks. "Yes I did...and it was worth the wait." She said it sort of defiantly. But her smile grew as did the reddening in her cheeks. "Good to know," I chuckled.

***

Dinner was quite an experience that evening. Just the three girls and me. Marissa was wearing a very nice tight fitting pair of jeans with a white transparent chiffon blouse that allowed a clear view of the black frilly bra she had on underneath. It was unbutton enough that I could see the top of her tits down to the top of her bra. She had her hair up in a bun like a librarian sort of look.

Katie was wearing some black cotton shorts that were so tight that I could see the camel toe in her crotch as she sat down to eat. Her long blonde hair had long springy curls that hung down along her face and neck. The black cotton blouse was not see-through but she had it tied in a loose knot just below her perky little tits and there were no buttons fastened.

I was surprised to see that Stevie was not wearing her combat boots. She was wearing a long flowing black lacy chiffon sort of dress. The sort of style you would imagine as a witches costume for Halloween. Except this was very sexy and very short. The front and rear sort of scooped down to cover her. But the sides were very high cut and I could see most of both her creamy white thighs.

"Doesn't Jake look good in his new shirt and jeans," Katie asked softly as we all sat down. "He looks fabulous, dear," Marissa told her. "You did a great job of helping him with his shopping," she added as she glanced up and down my body. "I was really disappointed that he wouldn't model his new thongs for me though," Katie laughed playfully.

"That's a shame, sissy," Stevie chuckled softly. She had that wry grin again. "He looks pretty hot in that gold and black tiger striped one he's wearing right now," she added smugly. Marissa and Kathleen both glared over at her in stark silence. "It's my fault," I blurted out. "I forgot to close my door while I was getting dressed." It was an attempt to bail her out. "You don't have to cover it up," Stevie smiled at me as she said it. "I peeked at you in the mirror to see what had my Mom all giggly about," she winked as she said it. "Gotta say...it made me giggly too," she laughed.

"So, that's why you're all dolled up this evening?" Katie sounded a bit miffed. I could see Marissa grinning as I glanced over at her. "Well, I sure as hell didn't dress nice for you," Stevie goaded her sister. There was another short silence that was interrupted by the sound of Charles the butler as he rolled in the cart with dinner. "Dinner is served Lady Marissa," he announced.

The dinner was divine! We had mouthwatering prime rib with baked potatoes, a vegetable medley and a tossed salad. But the dinner rolls were the best thing I had ever had. Each roll was like a mini loaf of French bread. "I could stay here forever just for these French rolls," I purred as I was about to eat my third one. They all sort of laughed at the same moment. "I had no idea you would be this easy to please," Marissa chuckled.

"Hey, I spent most of the last six years eating MRE's," I laughed. There was a silence until I realized that they had no clue what that meant. "Meals...Ready...to EAT," I spelled it out for them. "Sort of like a very nasty boxed lunch," I added. They were all grinning at me now. "But most of the fellas referred to them as Meals...Ready...to Excrete." I laughed at my own familiar joke.

Stevie nearly choked on her fork full of salad after I said it. "Oh, sorry!" I gasped. "I shouldn't be so vulgar at the dinner table," I mumbled my apology. "I've only been back for a month. I guess that I still have some rough edges," I added. Marissa reached over and placed her hand on my thigh.

"That's okay, Hun, we can all work on smoothing some of those out for you," she giggled. "Oh, Hell No!" Stevie blurted out. "I think he's fucking wonderful just the way he is." Marissa and Katie both burst into laughter over Stevie's outburst. "You're right, sweetie. He's wonderful just the way he is," Marissa laughed. "But don't let your father hear you using that kind of language in his house." she warned gently.

We spent several hours together in a large room that I would describe as a huge family room. We played scrabble and chatted and giggled a lot. It was a wonderful evening and all four of us got to know a little bit about each other.

I found that Kathleen was studying communications in college with the intention of becoming a TV News Journalist. Stevie will be starting her studies in literature in the fall with hopes of becoming a writer. Marissa confided that her family had just become affluent when she was in high school. Because of that she had gone through a long of period being outcast by her husband's family when they were first married. It was nearly midnight when I finally went back to my cottage. It had been a long day, but I had learned a lot and had many surprises.

Chapter 5

I was just crawling into bed when I heard the soft knock at my front door. I glanced at the clock and it was 1:32 a.m. "Come in, it's unlocked," I called from the hallway. It was Marissa that entered wearing a short white terrycloth robe. "Were you expecting someone?" she giggled as she came towards me. "Not really. But with the events of today I figured that someone might want in here before morning," I told her.

Marissa untied the belt and let her robe fall to the floor. She was wearing only a black thong underneath. "Recognize my panties?" she giggled. "They are the ones I had you leave in the cabana." Marissa was grinning from ear to ear. She informed me that she had been wearing them all night and had to bite her tongue when Stevie was bragging about seeing me in my thong at dinner. "I wanted to blurt out that I was wearing your thong at the table," she told me.

As Marissa was crawling into the bed, she informed me that she had told the girls to stay away for the night because Robert would be coming home tomorrow afternoon. She confided that her husband was planning to announce his candidacy for the open Senate seat this week and she would be required to be on his arm the entire week at the fundraiser events.

"I told the girls that they could keep you company during this time if they wish," she told me straight out. I was incredulous that she would be so okay with the idea of me banging her daughters. "I told them that they would have to work out their own schedule with you," she giggled. Marissa told me that she had work that would keep me busy during the days this week but I would have plenty of free time in the evenings while she and Robert were away at events.

"Now, take these panties off me and fuck me like you own me," she laughed wickedly as she held her arms open to me. I crawled onto the bed and slowly pulled the thong down till I had it off her feet. "Yessssss, Jake," she cooed as I bent forward and began eating her pussy. "Oh, God I wanted to fuck you at dinner," she moaned as she placed her hands on my head and pressed my face firmly against her sex.

For several minutes I swirled my tongue around her labia and gently teased her clit with just the tip until her body was squirming and vibrating on the bed. "Oooh, Fuck Yes," she moaned loudly when I scooted up and buried my dick in her drenched gash till I was buried to the balls. "Your cock feels s-o-o-o-o good," she groaned in a deep throaty voice.

Squish, Squish, Squish...Smack, Smack, Smack...her pussy was so sloppy wet that it was squirting little sprays of juice each time I pounded down onto her. The wetness made the slapping sounds even louder as I fucked her hard and savagely. "Ugh, Ugh, Ugh, Ugh..." she grunted forcefully each time I thrust into her. I had her wrists pinned up above her head as I shoved my dick into her as hard and fast as I could. "Take Me Baby, Take Me," she grunted.

I let go of her left wrist when I felt her starting to quiver near climax and moved the hand down to mash roughly on her right breast. As she began to jerk and shudder, I twisted savagely on her right nipple. "Ooooh, God yes, Jake...Ooooh, God Yes," she screamed. I shoved my dick as deep as it would go and ejaculated three huge wads of cum all over her cervix. "There you go, baby...there you go," I groaned.

We cuddled afterward for about twenty minutes before she got up to go back to the main house.

She informed me that Robert would be having a special invitation dinner and Ball here at the mansion on Saturday night for very rich friends and investors for his campaign. "I'm not sure if I will be able to get you invited," she told me. She left out the part about whether that was because I am banging her or because I am considered trailer trash to that group of people.

"I'll have one of the girls bring you breakfast in the morning," she told me as she was putting her robe on. "I can't really say if either one of them will ever fuck you, but I think they both are very enamored with your attention," she confided. "Either way, I think it will be good for both of them to experience those rough edges," she giggled. Marissa kissed me tenderly on the lips. "Stevie was absolutely right about you," she whispered an inch from my ear. "You are wonderful just the way you are, Jake."

***

"Mom was right, you have a gorgeous body," her voice startled me awake. I guess I must have stirred a bit when my body felt the pressure of someone sitting down on the bed next to me. I was still a bit groggy as I open my eyes to see Katie sitting there staring down at me. It took a few moments to remember that I was completely naked. I instinctively reached to pull the blankets up but found that they had been kicked off onto the floor at some point in my sleep.

"Should I lock the door from now on, or is it acceptable for me to be naked every time you barge into my house unannounced?" My voice was hoarse and strained. I could see a look of lust on her face as she gawked at my flaccid prick. "You can be naked any time I come over," she told me with her eyes never leaving my dick. "Besides, Mom told you I would be over for breakfast." I glanced at the clock and it was ten after 9am.

"Do you think I'm pretty, Jake?" She whispered. "Oh hell yes, Katie...you are so very sexy," I told her as I felt a slight wiggle. Kathleen was wearing that tiny white bikini again. The way she was seated with one leg dangling off the bed and the other leg bent beside her, left her legs spread wide apart and I could see her pussy lips pressed tight against the crotch of her bottoms.

"But, I'm so skinny and I have no tits," she complained softly. "Even Stevie has bigger tits than I have," she lamented. "Are you

yesterday," I confessed as she got me closer and closer to orgasm. "You made my pussy so wet when you were modeling those clothes," she answered me with a moan.

As I felt my load boiling up in my balls, my body went rigid and my head fell back onto my pillow.

"Cum for me, Jake...cum all over my titties," she moaned as she leaned forward so my dick was perched right in front of her breasts. "OOOOOH KATIE...OH GOD YES...OH FUCK YES," I screamed as I watched my semen spraying out all over her nubile little tits. I ejaculated four times and bathed her chest with a very messy load of my gooey seed. "That was really hot," she giggled as she smeared my semen all over her chest and throat.

"Oh geezus, you are sexy," I panted as I watched her put her top back on with my cum still smeared all over her. "Maybe next time I'll let you return the favor," she told me coyly as she got off the bed. "Oooh, God," I groaned as I watched her tight little ass jiggle while she walked to the door. "Enjoy your day, Jake," she giggled as she left.

I was kept very busy the rest of that day. Marissa had sent word that I should personally check all of the security cameras and all of the other security equipment since the mansion would be having so many high profile dignitaries arriving on Friday. I did see Marissa for a moment before lunch. "Katie told me you made quite a mess this morning," she whispered it so none of the staff could hear. "Yes, my rough edges seemed to really enjoy her smoothing effect," I joked. Marissa gave me a quick secret kiss on the side of my neck. "Keep up the good work," she giggled.

Although I was very busy after lunch, I noticed that the entire staff was scurrying around as they prepared for Robert's arrival. Charles took a few moments to discuss several hidden cameras that were not on the security plan diagram and told me it was paramount for me to not reveal their location to anyone else. "Not even the family members," he added secretly.

I found the first secret camera in Roberts's private library. The recording equipment was located in a secret panel behind a painting on the wall closest to his desk. The second secret camera was located in Marissa's private study. I felt a knot growing in my stomach as I remembered fucking Marissa on the couch in this room the day she hired me. The knot grew tighter when I found the third camera in the cabana where Marissa had sucked me off. I was feeling quite sick by the time I located the final camera in my cottage where I have had sex with Robert's wife and daughter. "Oh, Fuck me," I groaned as I sat down on my couch.

I received a call on my cell phone just before dinner time. "Did you check that equipment I suggested?" It was Charles on the other end. "Yes, I did...should I ...clean that equipment?" It was a coded way of asking if I should clear the recordings. "That won't be necessary, sir," Charles chuckled. "I just thought you should be aware of...this secret fascination." He said it very quietly. "But it will never be a concern," he added.

Although I felt a little better after the conversation, I still felt very uncomfortable with the situation. "Whose fascination is it?" I wondered. And why would it not be a concern for someone that went through all the trouble to install this equipment? Although my bathroom is out of sight from that camera, I still closed the door when I took my shower after I was finished with work. I had a deep feeling of dread the entire evening.

Chapter 6

I waited till a little before midnight when I was fairly sure that Marissa and Robert had gone to bed. Then I removed the camera memory chip so I could view what had been recorded recently on my laptop. I was relieved to find that the camera only recorded in the bedroom. But it still twisted my stomach into a knot as I watched myself banging the hell out of Marissa, and then Katie jerking me off on her tits. "How could this NOT be a concern?" I asked myself as I slipped the memory chip back into the camera.

It felt really creepy to me to go to sleep in the bedroom that night. The thought of that camera recording my every move made my skin crawl. I grabbed a blanket out of the hall closet and headed out to spend the night on the couch. It was just after 1 a.m. that I heard the front door creak open. "Who's there?" I yelled as I sat up. I had visions of a staff member coming over to beat me to a pulp on behalf of the boss. Just like when I was a trailer trash teenager.

"It's just me, silly." The soft girlie voice of Stevie informed me. "It's not safe for you to be here with me like this," I sort of whispered it so the camera couldn't hear me in the bedroom. "You must have found Daddy's secret toy," she giggled as she proceeded over to sit down next to me on the couch next to my legs. "Yes, I did," I blurted out. "And we shouldn't..." Stevie reached up and placed her hand over my mouth.

"It's okay, Jake, it's okay," she laughed as she pulled her hand back. "How on Earth can it be okay for your father to know that I am banging his wife and....playing with his daughters?" I gasped softly. "Because he has been banging the entire female staff for as long as I can remember," she whispered. "Because he has been in love with his press secretary, Joan, for many years," she confided. "And because Mom only stays with him to keep up his family appearance for the sake of his political ambitions." she concluded.

"In short, this is our way of rubbing his choices in his face," Stevie confessed in a whisper. "Knowing that he is sick enough to spy on us just makes us all very excited when we have had the opportunity to do something nasty for him to witness." She smiled as she said it. "Now, I heard you say that you assumed that I want to play with you," her little smirk returned.

"I don't assume that you want anything," I told her defensively. "I just thought with what happened this morning with Katie and...How you peeked at me yesterday...that was playing," I stammered. I pulled the covers up to hide the fact that I had a raging boner under the skimpy thong I was wearing. "I don't expect anything from you," I groused at her.

"Don't get your panties in a bunch," Stevie laughed with that smirk that she so often has. "I do want to play...a little," she whispered. "When I saw that mess you made all over Katie, it made me think of something that I would like." She said it in a teasing sort of way. "And what might that be?" I found myself curious as to what she might want.

"I have always wanted to watch a man jerk off and see the stuff spray out," she told me. "If I let you spray it all over my tits, would you do that for me?" she reached over to touch the lump in the blanket. "I can feel that you would like to," she giggled as her hand rubbed up and down on my throbbing prick. "Yessss, I'll do it for you, I'll do it," I gasped softly.

"Good, let's go to the bedroom then," she laughed as she stood up. "Oooh, Fuck Me," I groaned as she pulled her night shirt off and dropped it on the floor. She was completely exposed to me now except for the black boy short "cheeky" panties that she had on. And those were see-through enough that I could see her smooth pussy lips through the flimsy fabric.

"Oooh, Jake...look at that," she gasped as I pulled my thong off before climbing on the bed. "Katie was right. That's huge," she purred.

"Would you like to play with it like she did?" I asked while I reached over to get my lube out of the night stand. "Maybe next time...but this time I want to see you do it." Stevie's eyes were riveted to my twitching manhood. "That way I can imagine what you look like when you jerk off thinking about me," she teased me playfully.

I had Stevie sit on my thighs so that she can bend forward when I'm ready to unload. But the real reason was that I could see her better this way and I could feel her body trembling as she got more and more aroused. "You are so fucking sexy," I moaned as I began to stroke my dick with my well lubricated left hand. "It would thrill me if you would touch your titties for me," I whispered. "That way I can imagine you playing with yourself when I jerk off," I goaded.

"Yessss, baby," I purred when her hands moved up and she began to fondle herself. My dick did get much harder as I watched her playing with those yummy perfectly round grapefruit sized tits. To my delight she began humping back and forth as she became more aroused. My knuckles were now grinding up and down the crotch of her panties as I jerked off for her. Her panties were already soaking wet.

Once I realized that she was humping herself against my fingers, I timed my strokes so my knuckles would grind right into her gash each time she humped forward. I could hear that her breathing was now becoming ragged gasps for air as she got closer and closer to climax. I managed to wiggle one of my fingers enough so her panties pulled to the side and now her smooth slick pussy lips were humping up and down my knuckles. My hand was bathed with her flowing juices.

Suddenly, she stopped humping and she just pressed her pussy forcefully against my knuckles. "Don't stop, don't stop, Jake...please don't stop," she moaned in an unbelievably deep husky tone. As I quickened the pace of my jerking, her body suddenly jerked and her head fell back till she was staring up at the ceiling with her eyes rolled back into her head. "Oh My God, Jake, Oh My God...Oooooh My God."

As her body vibrated against my knuckles, I felt a gush of hot fluid spray out of her pussy. Then another and another. My entire fist, arm and belly were coated with her slick musky fluid as she began to fall forward. I began to ejaculate and the first blast shot all over her tits. But the following three ejaculations sprayed out all over her belly and mine as her body lay down on top of mine.

Stevie lay on top of me for several minutes as she panted for air. "That was fucking wonderful," she moaned hoarsely when she finally regained her bearings. "That feels so nasty," she giggled softly as she wiggled her belly back and forth against mine. The pool of cum trapped between us made a squishy noise as she did it. "That's yummy," she giggled.

***

The sensation of her bare pussy mashed against my prick felt delicious. "I think you should roll off me now," I whispered. "Before something happens that...you're not ready for yet." I could feel my dick wanting to slip inside of her slippery sex hole. Every part of my being wanted me to shove my dick up into her tight little cunt. But I knew that I should let her make that choice.

"Yes, maybe you're right," she whispered back. I felt her wiggle her pussy back and forth against my dick. "But you...would want...to fuck me?" Stevie asked softly. "Oh geezus, yes, I do, Stevie," I gasped. "You have no idea how desperately I want that," I added softly.

"Good!" she exclaimed. "Maybe sometime I'll let you," she giggled as she rolled off me and pulled her panties back over to cover her gash. I got one last glimpse of her pink glistening slit just before she yanked them back in place. "My god, you are sexy," I gasped. Stevie reached over and fondled my flaccid cock. "I'll think about this when I play with my pussy tonight," she told me with a playful grin. I could swear that she was looking directly at the hidden camera. "And I will think about your sexy titties and gushing pussy," I answered her.

I put some gym shorts on and walked out to the living room with her. It thrilled me to look at her nubile body for several more minutes before she pulled her nightshirt back on. "I am so flattered that you wanted to...spend this time with me," I confessed to her. "When we first met, I never dreamed that you might ever be interested in a fella like me," I told her

Stevie pushed me back till I was sitting on the couch then sat down on my lap with her legs straddling mine. "Just because I dress different and go out of my way to be a rebel doesn't mean I don't have girly desires," she laughed. She leaned forward and kissed me on the cheek. "You are just the first one that I have wanted to do something about it with," she told me as she stood up from my lap. "Who knows? Maybe I'll want some more," she giggled. My mouth was hanging wide open as she walked out my front door.

***

There was a knock on my front door at precisely 9 a.m. the next morning. Although I thought it might be one of the girls, I put my terry cloth robe on before I went to answer the door. I was a bit disappointed to find that it was Charles standing there with a food tray in hand. "Lady Marissa asked me to bring this for you," Charles informed me as he handed me the tray.

"Thank you for your help with my work list yesterday," I told him with a grin. "I found it very helpful even though it was a bit confusing," I added. "Maybe we can get together and discuss the details at your convenience," I suggested. Charles grinned slightly. "I will try to work that in sometime in a day or two," he answered me. "You have a good day, sir," he added.

***

There was a note underneath my plate of pancakes and eggs. *"Good morning, Hun. I hope you have a lovely day."* After her greeting, there was short list of chores that mostly would require me to walk the entire estate to ensure there were no safety issues or cosmetic concerns. It would be a fairly easy day and I would easily be done by lunch time.

I wore an old pair of my desert fatigue pants that day with my jump boots and a desert tan t-shirt. I was inspecting the front gate when Mr. Rhonan's limo approached from the mansion. The limo stopped next to me and the rear window slowly descended until it was all the way down and I could see inside the back.

"You must be, Jake?" Robert greeted me. "It's nice to have a war hero looking after our security," he told me. I could see a slight grin on Marissa's face as she sat there next to him in the back of the limo. "It is an honor to meet you Mr. Rhonan," I answered him. "I hope to be addressing you as Mr. Senator in the near future," I buttered him. I noticed Marissa's grin grow wider.

Robert flashed a killer smile as he turned to glance at Marissa. "I do love the respect of a serviceman," he told her. "I think you have chosen well," he added. "Perhaps we should invite him to the Ball?" he suggested. Robert turned back to look at me. "You DO still have your dress uniform?" he asked. "Yes Sir...it is hanging in my closet." I replied. "Good, that will look very nice at our formal event," he announced.

I could practically see the wheels turning in his brain. He could show off his Army grunt employee to all his investors and appear to be supporting the effort to hire Vets. "Good! It's all settled then. I will expect to see you around 9pm." As he drove away, I noted that he had NOT invited me for the dinner.

It was almost lunch time when I finally made it to the back of the estate. On my last sweep around the perimeter, I suddenly heard muffled moans coming from the cabana near the pool. I very quietly approached from behind. "Yeah baby, suck it good, suck it good," the male voice moaned softly.

Gluck, Gluck, Gluck, Gluck...I was stunned when I quietly pulled the curtain open a few inches to peer inside. Katie was on her knees completely naked sucking off her mother's chauffeur. "Yes baby, suck me off," he groaned. His head was pressed back against the wall and he was humping up into her mouth with both his hands on her head. I was surprised by the sudden flash of jealousy that bolted through me was I carefully let the curtain fall back into place.

"It's none of your business, Jake," I reminded myself as I quietly walked away. "HERE IT IS BABY, SUCK IT OUT OF ME," I heard the scream of his release. That was followed by the sound of gagging. And then it sounded like someone was vomiting. I just managed to get inside of the cottage before I saw Joey leaving the cabana. It was several minutes before I saw Katie come back out. Her hair looked wet like she had showered. The look on her face told me that this had not been an enjoyable experience.

Chapter 7

I was hugely disappointed when neither of the girls came over to visit me Tuesday evening. I felt a slight apprehension that maybe I have done something wrong. Perhaps Robert had taken exception to my playing with his daughters. Although I had not fucked either of them, I certainly had played with them sexually. Again, I felt that pang of jealousy about Katie blowing Joey in the cabana. Again, I reminded myself that it was none of my business. I also reminded myself that none of these women owe me a damn thing.

I lost all track of time on Wednesday. I was tasked with escorting the extra security crew around the grounds and reviewing all security measures since there were going to be many important dignitaries that would be attending the ball. The Governor would be attending as well as three Senators. So, I had to familiarize their security staff with the mansion and surrounding grounds

I did run into Stevie for a moment out by the garage while the security fellas were having lunch. I skipped that so I would have time to secure a loose roller on the garage door lifting trolley. "There you go teasing me," Stevie taunted me when she saw I was wearing fatigue pants and combat boots. "What can I say? I was trolling for a little rebel girl with girlie intentions," I teased her back. The sound of her girlish laughter made my heart flutter. I noticed that her round little ass swished a little more as she walked away. She looked so damn sexy in those cutoff fatigue shorts and combat boots.

It was well after dinner time when I finally got back to my cottage. It was already half past 9 p.m. as I pulled off my boots. I decided that I would take a quick shower and then make something in the microwave for dinner. I dropped my clothes on the floor in the hallway and climbed into the nice warm water.

"Did I mention that you are the most gorgeous man I have ever seen?" I was just rinsing the soap out of my hair when Stevie's unexpected voice startled me. "Damn girl, don't you ever knock?" I gasped loudly. I tend to yell when I'm startled. When I turned to face her, she was directly in front of me staring at my naked body through the sliding glass door.

"Do you always get hard like that around girls?" Stevie murmured as I bent over to turn off the water. Her eyes were riveted to my now rigid prick. "Yes, that tends to happen whenever I am naked in front a gorgeous girl," I chuckled. I heard her shrieking as I rolled open the sliding door.

"You think I'm gorgeous!" she squealed as she threw herself into my arms. It took all of my balance to not fall back into the tub as she kissed the side of my neck. "What can I say? I have a real weakness for a girl in combat boots," I chuckled when she finally let go and stepped back.

Stevie pulled off her t-shirt over her head and tossed it on the floor. "I told you the other night that I might want some more." She said it coyly. "If you're interested, I'll be on the bed." My dick was twitching as I watched her saunter to my room in her shorts and boots. "Damn!" I gasped. I had to chuckle when I entered the bedroom and saw Stevie sprawled across my bed in just her pink transparent bikini panties. "What's so funny?" she asked in an alarmed tone. "It's nothing," I smiled down at her as I approached the bed and dropped my towel. "I was just enjoying your girliness," I chuckled again.

"Maybe you should take those off so you don't they don't get ruined," I suggested as I crawled onto the bed next to her. Stevie raised her hips and grinned. "Go ahead, take them off," she told me softly. My hands were trembling as I very slowly pulled her panties down to her feet and then off. I reached up and hung them on the bed post.

"And what did you have in mind Miss Sassy Boots?" Stevie burst out laughing. "I love that! Sassy Boots...hahahaha...Sassy Boots."

Again, her laughter made my heart flutter in my chest. "Could you lick me...down there?" she requested very softly. "I would love to, sweetie," I replied without hesitation. I slowly crawled between her legs and lowered my face to her smooth little slit.

"Oooooh, Jake," she moaned softly as I took my first swipe all the way up her gash with my drooling tongue. Stevie had the sweetest pussy I ever tasted and I could feel copious amounts of precum oozing out of my prick onto the bed as I swirled my tongue around inside of her tight little sex hole.

"Oooooh Jake, Oooooh Jake," she moaned as I found her little clit and began attacking it with quick darting flicks of my tongue. When I felt her hands grab ahold of my head, I started to suck on her little pearl and gently nibble on it with my teeth. Stevie's body suddenly arched up and she let out a howl as she convulsed into climax. My mouth was flooded with her nectar, the sweet musky scent of her sex filled my nostrils.

Stevie's body continued to quiver and shudder for several moments as I crawled up next to her.

Little aftershocks coursed through her belly as she moaned softly. "That was incredible, Jake," she panted hoarsely. "So, you might be wanting some more of that?" I teased.

"Oooh Yes, Jake...Oh, God yes." she purred.

"What's THIS?" Stevie giggled as she wrapped her hand around my painfully rigid prick. "I know how to fix thaaaaat," she teased. As she scooted up and sat her naked body on top my thighs, I thought that she would probably jerk me off like last time. "Yessss, baby," I purred.

Stevie slowly raked the head of my dick against her dripping wet gash. "I told you that you're the only man I have ever wanted to do this with," she whispered. "Oooh, Stevie. What....are you doing?" I gasped when she pressed forward so that the mushroom head of my cock burrowed between her pussy lips. "I'm giving you my cherry, Jake," she groaned as she shoved forward till my entire dick was lodged inside her incredibly tight virgin cunt.

"Gaaaaawwwwwd, that's huge," she groaned. Stevie shuddered for several long moments as she sat there motionless impaled on my 9 inch dick. The three inches of girth stretched her virgin pussy canal like a balloon ready to burst. I could feel the warm slippery fluid of her hymen oozing down onto my thighs. "Wow, Jake...it's so big," she groaned

"Oh Stevie, Fuck that's tight," I moaned my reply. Her tight little pussy was squeezing my cock so hard that I could feel every pulse of my heart in the head of my dick. "I will never forget this,

Stevie...I will never forget this," I panted. My eyes were drinking in every inch of her luscious naked body as she sat there quivering. "Damn, you are gorgeous," I moaned hoarsely.

"Ooooh Jake, Ooooh Jake," she moaned as she began to hump up and down on my rigidness. "That feels so good, Jake...s-o-o-o-o good." Her hands were straight down on my chest and her fingernails were digging into my skin. But the exquisite sensation of her hot sex squeezing my dick was so delicious that I could barely feel the pain of her scratching fingers.

Slap, Slap, Slap, Slap...Stevie's firm round ass cheeks smacked down against my thighs as she increased the force and speed of her thrusts. Her tight little hole felt so fucking good as it milked my throbbing pipe that I barely made it two minutes till I felt the twinge in my sack that told me that the happy ending was near.

"Stevie, you better stop...you better...OOOH STEVIE...OOOOH GOD....OOOOH MY GOD." My legs were jerking uncontrollably as my cock erupted deep into her virgin womb. "Oooh Stevie, Ooooh Stevie," I screamed as she continued to ride me like a prize bull. "YESSSS, YESSSS, YESSSS," she screamed her answer as she finally reached her orgasm too.

I was a little concerned as she rolled off me and cuddled up by my side. It worried me that I had just flooded her virgin womb with a huge load of little baby makers and she was probably not on the pill. But as she gently kissed my neck and whispered my name, it all melted away. We fell asleep twisted together like a pretzel.

***

I awoke briefly at about 4am to find that Stevie had left to go back to the main mansion. For a split second, I almost thought that maybe tonight had been a dream. My eyes fell upon her pink panties hanging from my bedpost and I smiled a sweet smile of satisfaction. Stevie really did give me her virginity this evening.

I felt a pressure next to me on the bed as the sun was just dawning. "I had hoped to bed you first, but it looks like sissy got there first." I opened my eyes to see Katie sitting next to me. She was nude and the soft light of the rising sun glowed across her perky little tits. I could feel my dick swelling as she bent forward to tenderly kiss my lips.

"And would you have me still?" I whispered as I reached up to gently brush my fingers across her breasts. "Yesssssss," she purred. I slowly raked my finger down her belly and down between her legs. "Oooooh, Jake," she moaned when I hooked my middle finger up into her wet slit.

"Are you sure you want this?" I whispered. "I think that Stevie has plans of a more permanent nature," I confided. "Take Me, Jake. Taaaaake Me," she groaned as I wiggled my finger against her aroused clit. I rolled Katie onto her back and very slowly inched my dick into her pussy till I was buried to the bone. Katie had a wonderfully lustful grin on her face as I slowly pulled out and then slid into her again. "Ooooooh, Jake," she cooed.

I lifted up with my arms so I could gaze at her deliciously slender nubile body. "You are so fucking pretty," I whispered as I slowly drove myself into again. Although she was not quite as tight as her little sister, her skinny little body felt marvelous with my cock stretching her sex beyond anything she had ever experienced. "Oooh Jake, Oooh Jake," she moaned.

I hooked my leg around Katie and rolled onto my back so she would now be perched on top with her still impaled on my prick. "Fuck me, Katie...Fuck me," I groaned as I raised my head to suck on her cone shaped tits. Her puffy nipples felt divine as I swirled my tongue around one and then the other. The sound of her pounding down onto my thighs echoed in my small room.

When I felt her body quivering while she slammed down harder and harder, I could tell that she was close to her orgasm but just couldn't quite get over the edge. I moved my right hand down to the crack of her ass and began to rub little circles around her anus.

"Oooh Jake, Oooh Jake," she moaned in a throaty voice.

I slowly slipped the tip of my middle finger into her little rosebud and wiggled it gently. "OH MY GOD JAKE, OH MY GAAAAAAWWWWWD," she screamed as her body twisted and vibrated uncontrollably. My cock erupted inside of her flooding her with my seed. While we were resting,

Katie told me that Stevie had told her that she would be okay with sharing me with Katie and her Mother. But she added that she intended to be my number one.

Katie was just leaving when Stevie arrived with my breakfast. "Mom says that you can have today's off," she announced. "She wants you at your peak performance for the ball tonight." Stevie winked and added, "I don't think she has dancing in mind."

As I ate my waffles and sausage links, Stevie informed me that she intended to have babies with me. Then she announced that it would be okay for me to visit with her sister and her mom from time to time.

"And how is all of this going to happen?" I chuckled. "Right after you marry me, silly." She laughed.

The End

Here is a sample from another story you may enjoy:

Hot Erotica

BLACKMAILED
NANNY

SERVICING THE HELP

JACK RYDER

To some people, I guess that you could say that I was born into a life of privilege; a life of financial privilege that is. Dad had made a killing at the very beginning of the computer boom of the early 90's. I was 6 years old when we moved from the suburbs of Los Angeles to our mansion north east of Seattle. Although we were not as rich as the old money millionaires from out east in the Hamptons, Dad's wealth was just beginning to amass. By the time I was ten, he was a billionaire several times over.

Even though our wealth was what you would call "new money", Mom and Dad quickly settled into the lifestyle of the rich and famous. This meant that we now had maids and butlers to take care of the mansion. We had limos with chauffeurs to take us everywhere and anywhere we wanted at any time we wanted. My baby sister Phoebe and I even had a nanny.

Gracie was only 18 when Dad hired her to be our surrogate mother, so to speak. That was really what she was for us since Mom got so busy with her civic duties and private clubs. From the moment that Dad struck it rich; it was like our parents never again had more than a few minutes alone with us. The both of them did try to compensate for this by throwing money and gifts at Phoebe and me but Gracie who ended up becoming our only adult supervision.

At the time, I could never figure out why Gracie stayed with us all these years. From the start, Phoebe was a high maintenance child with an assortment of physical maladies and mental health issues and although I was much better equipped to take care of my own needs, I was an absolute hellion when I was a young preteen.

I constantly found little pranks to pull on Gracie. Rearranging furniture in rooms after she had set things right, adding extra soap to the laundry so it would bubble over. Rearranging things on my father's study desk after she had placed everything exactly the way he wanted them. I could only imagine what hell I put her through back then. After I reached puberty, it got even worse for her. I began peeping on her in the shower and in her bedroom when she was getting dressed. However, by the time I reached high school, it was a little better for her. Phoebe's psychologist had finally found a combination of medications that made Phoebe much more manageable and I had let up on the pranks. Now, my main interest was finding ways to see Gracie in the nude and taking secret photos of her with either my cell phone or the fancy professional type camera that Mom had given me as a birthday gift.

I guess that you could say that I sort of had a crush on my nanny at this point. Although she was twelve years older than me, she was the prettiest woman I had ever seen. Even though I had plenty of girls at school who were willing to throw themselves at me because my father's wealth, Gracie was the only woman I ever fantasized about. She was the only girl that interested me.

With the way I treated her when I was a kid; I could not understand why she didn't simply quit. Dealing with my family was hard enough for me; I could only imagine what it was for her. I was even more shocked that Gracie stayed with us for so long after I saw exactly what my father was demanding of her. It was just after my 18th birthday and about three weeks before I was going to graduate from high school. I came home from school much earlier than usual that day and Dad happened to be home from one of his many month-long business trips.

I heard soft voices coming from the study as I came up the stairs to my room. "Yes baby...you know what I want..."

If you enjoyed this sample then look for **Blackmailed Nanny.**

Here is another sample you may also enjoy:

The narrow village road looked the same. Nothing had changed since she left a few years ago. Time had left her home village behind. There were no new houses and the old ones were just as she remembered them, each set back away from the road and surrounded by flowering bushes and fruit trees.

No one was out and about at this time of day. Most of the villagers would be tending their vegetable plots and rice fields. Anna walked to a small wooden house raised five feet above the ground on short, stout timber beams.

She took off her shoes and using the dipper, scooped water from the big urn next to the steps and washed her feet, the way all the villagers did before entering their homes.

She climbed up the six steps, crossed the small verandah to the closed door. It was not locked. None of the villagers had cause to lock their homes. Everyone knew everybody and strangers never pass their way. It was as if their village had been forgotten and it remained as it had always been. Simple wooden houses were built raised off the ground in case the heavy monsoon rains caused the small stream running by the village to overflow and flood the surroundings. There were no fences, only well-worn paths leading off to the twenty or so homes, each well-tended and boasting a variety of flowering shrubs, potted plants and fruit trees.

Anna walked into the small living room. All was quiet except for the cat that purred, opening her eyes as she sensed Anna.

"Putih!" Anna called out and the cat padded over to her, rubbing its head against Anna's bare ankles.

Anna carried her small suitcase into the back room. It had not changed. The single bed with a dresser next to the window, was neatly made. The wooden chair beside the bed was still there. On it sat the cushion embroidered with a prowling tiger. The tiger stared at her, its eyes probing her innermost secrets. The cushion was one of a set of two. She had bought the set as the tiger embodied a life-changing experience for her and Song. She had given the other cushion to Song as a potent reminder of how close they came to be a meal for the tiger. Song, his name threatened to push her into places she had no wish to revisit.

She had come home. This was the room of her childhood and adolescence, her refuge from the storms that had ripped her life apart at a tender age. Her grandparents had taken her in and raised her in this little village ever since she was five.

She looked at the photographs hanging on the wall. There were three altogether.

One showed Anna as a young child with her parents, Zul and Ainee.

The second showed Anna in school uniform clutching a trophy, flanked by her beaming grandparents.

The third showed Anna alone, with the iconic Petronas Twin Towers of Kuala Lumpur in the background.

Her life history depicted by these three photographs left big blanks that strained the curiosity of those who had come to know Anna and visited her village home.

The dream did not fade over time, not like her grandma had said it would. She used to wake up screaming, cowering in fear and her grandma would rush in and hold her, rocking her gently, murmuring words of love and assurance until her sobs subsided into hiccups and she fell asleep in Grandma's arms.

As she grew older, she learned to stifle her screams with her pillow and not wake her grandparents because they had to get up early to tend to their rice field about half a kilometer away from their village.

The first photograph triggered sketchy memories of her parents.

Her mother was a beautiful woman with big flashing eyes and red lips that often parted in a wide smile. Her father was short, like her grandfather, but had broad shoulders. Anna remembered his strong arms whenever he lifted her into the air and she would scream in delight. She also remembered the big fights whenever mama came home late and there was no dinner on the table for papa, no dinner for Anna, who had been alone in the flat when papa unlocked the front door.

If you enjoy this sample then look for **The Red Peony by Denise Denton.**

Also by this Author:

The Handyman Seduction

The Beer Bust Scandal

Scandalous Emotion

Intimate Relation

The Seduction of Kimi

Erotic Goes Hi-Tech

One at a Time

The Wizard Casey's Coven

The Inn Keeper's Wizard: When Love and Magic Collide

Trailer Trash Payback

Queer Intentions

Zoe's Fun House

Public Display

Test Drive

Breaking the Bonds

Trailer Trash Payback

The Hero's Welcome

The Twenty-Eight Day Cure

The Cougar Club

The Wife Swap

In Love with a Cougar

Stella for Christmas

The Long Ride Home

A Shot at Love

My Swedish Greta

The Second Honeymoon

Candy's Playmate

Sara's House of Hands

Loving My Sitter

His Wife and Her Husband

Bi-Curious Couple

Take Three, Mr. Writer

Blackmailed Nanny

About the Author

Jack Ryder LOVES everything there is about sex!

When he is not involved with his "swinger" friends, enjoying a steamy threesome, or being part of a raunchy "gang bang", you can find him on first class planes, trains, and cruise ships. Traveling seems to be the BEST way to finding new and interesting sexmates for him. Sexmates. Plural. He lives with the saying "The More, The Merrier!"

He owns a successful business in New York. He writes as a hobby and also as sort of documentation of his mind-blowing sexcapades over the years. He is presently roaming around the streets of Manhattan but can be anywhere in the world too, since he travels often. So, beware! You just might be his next mate.

The most fun thing I enjoy when writing my stories is trying to figure out which is fantasy and which was memory. ENJOY! (Preferably with a friend. *wink*) " -Jack Ryder-

From the Author

If you have any comments, suggestions, or would just like to get a little personal, please feel free to email me at:
jack_ryder@awesomeauthors.org

If you enjoyed any of my books then please share the love and click like on my books in Amazon.

If you write me a review and send me an email I will send you a free book, or many.
(Just know that these emails are filtered by my publisher.)

Good news is always welcome.

One Last Thing, For Kindle Readers...

When you turn the page, Kindle will give you the opportunity to rate this book and share your thoughts on Facebook and Twitter. If you enjoyed my writings, would you please take a few seconds to let your friends know about it? Because... when they enjoy they will be grateful to you and so will I.

Thank You!

Jack Ryder
jack_ryder@awesomeauthors.org